Shanna and the Pentacle

An Ostara Story

by Arie Farnam

Illustrations by Julie Freel

ISBN-13: 978-1530503612
ISBN-10: 1530503612

DEDICATION

To Marik, Shaye amd Ember

CONTENTS

Chapter One

Devil Worshipper

Ten-year-old Shanna touched her necklace with her left hand. Her little brother Rye gripped her right. It was their first day at a new school. The building was yellow but the cement and pale dead grass around it looked unfriendly and barren to Shanna.

Momma honked her horn and waved from the car. Their new house was close enough to walk from, but they had been nervous about the first day so Momma drove them. Now she had to hurry to work and couldn't even come in the building. They had come the day before just to see their new classrooms, so Shanna knew where to go. But that didn't make it entirely comfortable.

Big fat pink earthworms, like the ones Momma was so excited about having in their new backyard, seemed to be crawling around in Shanna's stomach. She wished her best friend Skylar was going to school with her. She wished it so hard that her mouth tasted bitter.

1

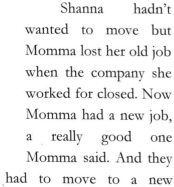

Shanna hadn't wanted to move but Momma lost her old job when the company she worked for closed. Now Momma had a new job, a really good one Momma said. And they had to move to a new town, with a new house and a new school. Shanna wasn't at all sure any of it was a good thing.

She had to leave her old school and her friends behind. When they left, Skylar had given her a special necklace and showed her the one she had just like it. She said they would be friends forever, even if they had to talk on the phone instead of passing notes in class. Skylar had made Shanna promise to wear her friendship necklace all the time and come back to visit as soon as she could.

The necklace was really pretty. It had an obsidian black pentacle with a little silver vine wound around it. It was strung on a leather cord that felt warm and comforting when Shanna curled her fingers around it.

Now she rubbed the pretty vine for luck and started toward the door to the school. There were five cement steps and a wheelchair ramp off to the side. Otherwise the building was a large block, not a small, cozy building like their school back home.

Other kids were walking in and some of them glanced at Shanna and Rye but no one really seemed to notice they were new. At their old school, if someone was new, everyone stared. Here the school was so big, Shanna wasn't even sure anyone would notice two new kids. That was actually a bit of a relief.

Shanna walked in past the front office where they had registered and down the long hallway where the first and second-grade classrooms were. Rye was in second, having just turned eight in the winter. When she left him, Rye peered back at her from the doorway with wide, brown eyes.

For once he wasn't grinning and goofing around. Up until now, he'd treated the whole moving thing like it was a great adventure. Now he'd see.

Shanna turned at the end of the hallway and climbed the steps to the upper grades. The other kids were starting to run now, sprinting around her and dashing down the hall.

The kids were another thing that was different about this school. They came in all shades of brown—from milky pale to dark brown. Momma was excited about that. She said it was great for Shanna and Rye to go to a "diverse" school and learn about other people. Shanna wasn't so sure.

By the door to her fifth-grade classroom, a clump of girls was whispering and passing around a tattered notebook. As she approached, they looked up and giggled behind their hands

"You must be the new kid," a girl with straight light brown hair said. Her hands were planted on her hips as if she was ready to challenge Shanna to something and she smacked her gum.

"I guess," Shanna said.

"I'm Brandy," the girl said and nodded around at her friends with a smirk, but didn't introduce them. "If you want anything you just let me know. The school 'friendliness rule' and all that."

She sneered on the last sentence, her lip curling up as she turned toward the door.

"Hi, I'm Shanna," Shanna said, even though they mostly had their backs turned to her now, following Brandy.

One of the girls glanced quickly back at Shanna. She was one of the really dark girls, her skin the color of the unsweetened chocolate that made Shanna's tongue want to curl up from the bitterness. The girl's eyes flashed at Shanna— almost smiling— but then she jerked them away and didn't say anything as she followed the other girls inside.

Shanna walked in behind them as a harsh buzzer went off

in the hallway, but then she had to stand by the door uncomfortably for a long time. The teacher was writing something on the blackboard and Shanna didn't know where she was supposed to sit.

Finally the teacher saw her and smiled with friendly little crinkles at the corners of her eyes. "You're Shannon or Shanna?" She asked, shuffling some papers. "Silver?"

"Yeah," Shanna said, carefully not looking at the kids, who were rustling in their seats and probably staring at her. "Just Shanna."

"Welcome, Shanna," the teacher looked up and smiled again while she brushed a stray gray hair out of her face. "My name is Mrs. Baker. Please sit in the free seat next to Rebecca."

Rebecca turned out to be the black girl who had glanced back at Shanna. She looked up through her eyelashes and almost smiled again but not quite. She kept looking toward Brandy and the other girls.

The girl in the seat behind Shanna's grinned at her though, a flash of braces glinting off her teeth. She had wildly curly black hair and big colorful earrings. Her skin was somewhere in the middle between the really dark kids and the really pale kids.

Shanna smiled back at her. She was glad to have someone happy to see her at last.

Their first subject was reading, right after the teacher asked for homework to be turned in and made an announcement about an Easter program. Shanna already felt lost. She didn't know what they were doing in any of their subjects and it felt like she would never fit in.

They had a short break in the middle of the morning and Shanna was about to get up to go get a drink of water, but Brandy pushed through two of the boys in the next aisle and came up to Shanna really fast. She stuck her hand out and snapped her fingers under Shanna's chin.

"Well, let me see?" she demanded. And before Shanna could react, Brandy's hand closed around her pentacle necklace.

"That's it!" one of the other girls said. "I told you so, Brandy. You remember they showed that in Sunday school. She's a devil worshipper."

Brandy stared at the pendant for a moment and then

gave it a yank as if testing to see if the leather cord would break. When it didn't, she dropped the necklace back against Shanna's chest and pretended to wipe her hand off on her skirt.

"I was going to let you sit with us at lunch, since you're new and all," she said. "But first you'd have to tell us what that is."

Shanna swallowed hard. There were now at least four girls standing around her. They weren't even trying to be quiet. Rebecca had turned around to stare at Shanna as well and every trace of her almost-smile was gone.

"It's just a necklace from my friend," Shanna said.

"Yeah, I'll bet," Brandy said. "Your friend Satan. That's a devil sign. I've seen it before. We're always vig-il-ant." She said the last word like it was three words or she didn't know exactly what it meant.

Shanna put her hand over the pentacle necklace. She hoped they wouldn't try to break it. Tears stung the back of her eyelids and her belly felt like it had a big round hole in it.

Brandy whirled around and walked away with a bouncy stride, saying to the air around her, "We'll just see about this."

The other girls and even some of the boys were staring at Shanna now. One of the girls looked really horrified with her hand over her mouth.

Another one was smiling a little and she said, "You'll go to hell and get burned to a crisp, you know."

Then the boys started laughing and the girls turned around and walked after Brandy. Even Rebecca got up and went after them.

Shanna walked toward the door with her head down, not looking at anyone. Her mouth was so dry now it hurt her throat and she needed to get to the water fountain.

But before she got to the door, Mrs. Baker said, "Shanna, please come here a minute."

Shanna stopped and turned, walking toward the teacher's desk. The front of the room smelled of chalk and glue. Shanna looked up and smiled at Mrs. Baker. She remembered how her old teacher Ms. Durrett had put a stop to kids laughing at each other. Shanna didn't want to complain about it, but the teacher had to have heard the mean things the other girls had said. Surely, she would stop them, if Shanna just kept quiet.

"My class is fairly advanced in math and spelling," Mrs. Baker said. "Would you look back at the last few lessons to make sure you're caught up?"

Shanna nodded, even though her stomach dropped a little. Mrs. Baker's eyes were still kind, despite her somewhat frazzled appearance.

"Come and talk to me if you have any trouble," she said. "And, Shanna, I hope you like our school. Everyone can get along here as long as we all make an effort."

The teacher's soft gray gaze suddenly sharpened and she pointed a long finger directly at Shanna's necklace.

"However, I will have to ask you to take that off right now. I won't have disruptive things or symbols of evil in my classroom," she said with a clipped tone. "I expect I won't see it at school again or anything similar."

Shanna felt like somebody really big was squeezing her throat. She reached up with a numb hand and closed it protectively around her friendship necklace.

"Did you hear me?" the teacher demanded.

"Yeah... er... yes, I did," Shanna said.

"Well, take it off then," the teacher said. "You'll find that you fit in better if you don't try to be too special."

Shanna was so confused that she forgot to get a drink and she walked back toward her desk. Her cheeks were on fire. Most of the other kids were quiet, waiting to see what she would do. The pressure of tears was growing in the corners of her eyes, but she bit the inside of her cheek and swallowed to make them go away.

She reached her desk and sat back down in her chair. She lifted the necklace carefully over her head and coiled the leather thong around the silver vine and put it into her pocket.

When Shanna didn't do or say anything else, whispers started back up all around the room. The kids were getting their coats on now and streaming toward the door for the outside break. Shanna wondered if she could just stay inside but then she thought about being in the quiet room with Mrs. Baker and she started to stand up again.

A gentle hand tapped her elbow and Shanna turned to see the smiling face of the girl with the colorful earrings.

"Do you want some gum?" the girl asked. "It's orange."

The girl held out a package of gum and Shanna wondered if it was some kind of trick. Sometimes kids play tricks on another kid who they don't like. But Shanna glanced up and no one else was watching.

"Okay, thanks," she said. Gum might help to make her throat feel better. The girl slid one piece out and Shanna put it in her mouth. The sweet citrus taste immediately made her think of sunshine and she felt a little better.

But then she noticed something. This girl wore a necklace too with a pendant not that different from Shanna's.

Except hers was on a gold-colored chain and it wasn't a pentacle. It was a tall, shiny cross.

Something about it made Shanna feel cold. When Rye asked what a cross on a building was, Momma said it was a church. Momma told Shanna to be quiet and respectful when

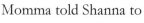

they went inside a church because it was a "sacred space" like their altar at home.

Shanna thought a cross must be a lot like a pentacle, but the teacher wouldn't let Shanna wear her necklace while this girl could wear her cross. It wasn't fair. Suddenly the gum didn't taste so good anymore.

"I'm Ella," the girl said. "Is your name Shanna?"

Now Shanna noticed that the girl spoke a little differently, as if she put a lot of Ys before her vowels. Shanna thought maybe she knew another language.

"Yeah," Shanna felt so sad that she didn't feel like saying any more.

Chapter Two

A New Beginning

When school was over, Shanna met Rye in the lower hallway and they walked out together. The air outside smelled good after the stuffy school building. The earth was damp and fresh from a sprinkling of rain. The muddy brown of the grass on the playground was now speckled with tiny bits of bright green where blades of new grass pushed up through the packed earth. Shanna even saw a bird making a nest in a tree by the swings.

Momma was waiting for them outside the school. Her smile was wide and her arms enveloped both kids in a hug. Momma smelled wonderful, like the flowery, herbal soap she made. And now she smelled like ink and a bit of oil too. Only faintly, not in an unpleasant way.

"How was your first day, brave explorers?" she asked, peering first at one of them and then at the other.

"Okay," Rye said. He shrugged but he was still grinning. He was almost always cheerful, no matter what happened. "I know all the math they're doing and my teacher said my drawing was really good. I drew a mountain for the science picture."

"That's wonderful, Rye," Momma said. "I'll bet you're proud of yourself, doing so much on your first day."

Rye wiggled inside his jacket as he climbed into the back seat of the car. Momma gave Shanna an extra squeeze and she got in too.

"Yeah, it was okay," Rye said. "But some kids laughed at me and said I draw like a girl. I don't want to sit next to them."

Momma blinked at Rye in the rearview mirror as she started the car. "How can someone draw like a girl?" she asked.

Rye screwed up his nose the way he did when he was thinking. "I don't know. I guess they think all drawing is for girls. None of the other boys would draw for the science

project."

"Hmmm…" Momma murmured. "Is that so? What do you think?"

"I like drawing," Rye said. "I don't think it's fair if only girls get to draw. And my teacher said it's not true."

"It's good that you know what you think," Momma said. "Sometimes people won't agree with you. You have to be strong and keep what you love anyway."

When they got home, Shanna helped Momma carry groceries into the house. Their yard was even worse than the school playground. It was overgrown with dried up dead weeds from the winter. Inside there were still boxes from their move piled all along the wall in the hallway and on the floor in the kitchen. Shanna thought Momma would start unpacking again, but instead she got out some elderberry syrup and made them each a drink of tangy sweet water with it. Then she sat down and smiled at Shanna.

"So, how was your day, Shanna?" she asked. "Do you like the new school?"

Shanna didn't want to make Momma worried. She knew Momma had a lot of work with the move and her new job.

So, all she said was, "Some kids laughed at me too and my teacher isn't all that nice either."

Momma looked more serious and she waggled her fingers for Shanna to come over to her. Then she gave her a sitting down hug. "Honey, I know it isn't going to be easy. Starting new things is hard. If it doesn't get better we'll find a way to make it better. You can always tell me what's happening and we'll talk to your teacher if we have to. Can you try a few days to see if it gets better?"

"Sure. Okay," Shanna said, but she didn't feel all that sure.

She put her pentacle necklace on again at home, but then in the morning she put it in her pocket to go to school. She could reach inside and feel it and think of Skylar, but her heart felt heavy.

Shanna and Rye walked to school that day and Shanna got to her classroom a few minutes early. Ella was already at her desk, bent over something small in her hand, but she looked up and waved when she saw Shanna.

Shanna couldn't help smiling back. Ella had another pair of earrings on. This time they were sparkly. They looked like they were made out of little wires twisted into spirals and curlicues.

"Those are pretty earrings," Shanna said.

Shanna and Skylar used to have a game where they would see how many true but nice things they could find to say to other people in

their class.
And it became a kind
of habit, so Shanna always
gave people random
compliments.

"Oh, thanks!" Ella said, her hand going up to touch one of her earrings. "I made them. They aren't perfect though. I want to make some more when I get done with my bike."

Shanna was confused. What did earrings have to do with a bike? And how could you make earrings by yourself anyway?

Ella held up the small thing she had in her hand in explanation. It was a tangle of little curled wires. In her other hand she had a pair of needle-nose pliers.

Shanna sat down on her chair backward and looked at the thing in Ella's hand. It wasn't just a mass of wires after all. They were all twisted in spirals and patterns to make what might be a broken bicycle.

"You're missing the back wheel," Shanna giggled.

Ella started laughing too. "Not for long. I just have to finish the pedals and then I'll do the wheel."

For a few minutes Shanna watched Ella twist another little wire into place to make a perfect miniature pedal.

"I'll teach you how to do it, if you want," Ella said. "I love making things. Do you want to come over to my house on Saturday?"

"I have to paint eggs with my mom on Saturday," Shanna said.

"You mean for Easter?" Ella asked with a bit of excitement.

Shanna shrugged. Even the kids back home who she had told about Imbolc didn't know about Ostara. No one ever knew about Shanna's holidays at school. And she was starting to get a feeling that it might not be a good idea to mention them here. At her old school, Tony had said Shanna's holidays were made up, but the teacher there wouldn't let anyone say mean things. Mrs. Baker hadn't stopped Brandy and the other girls from calling Shanna a "devil worshipper," and Shanna didn't think she would stop anyone if they laughed at her different names for holidays either.

Ella kept right on talking though, so Shanna didn't have to answer.

"I haven't painted eggs yet," she chattered. "We came here three years ago. Last year I wanted to paint eggs but my mom didn't know how. We don't do that in Guatemala. I hope we can do it in school. They did it in school when I was in third grade, but I was sick that day."

"I could show you how," Shanna said. She was still nervous but she couldn't help it. Ella sounded so happy and bubbly.

Ella looked up from her work and grinned. "Thanks. I really would like to."

"I'll ask my mom if you can come on Saturday and paint eggs with us, okay?" Shanna said. "That way you can show me how you make things with wires too."

"Okay," Ella said.

Chapter Three

Mud Fight

Shanna felt a lot better after talking to Ella. It was like the sun had come out from behind a cloud. The bell rang and Mrs. Baker came in to start the class.

At recess that morning, Ella and Shanna went outside together. The tiny green buds on all the tree branches made the trees and bushes look like fuzzy balls, if you squinted at them. The pale, bright green of new leaves and grass was everywhere, creeping over the brown mud of winter like a pretty clean blanket. There were even a few bright yellow buttercups poking up along the playground fence.

The two girls sat on the swings talking and breathed in the earth and leaf smells. Shanna could hear the bird chirruping in its nearby nest.

After a little while, a boy who sat across from Ella in class came up and said, "Hi." He had short, shiny hair and his skin was even darker than Ella's but not deep brown like Rebecca's.

"How's your bike?" he asked Ella.

"Almost done," Ella said, and she pulled the wire bicycle out of her purse to show him.

"That's really cool," he said.

"He's Rohan," Ella said, grinning mischievously. "He's pretty nice for a boy."

"What do you mean 'for a boy,'" the kid named Rohan laughed. "You're smart for a girl, since you can make bikes out of wire."

Ella kicked gravel at his shoe. "I'm going to teach Shanna how to do it. Girls are way smarter than boys. And nicer too."

"They are not," Rohan was still grinning at Ella. Shanna could tell they really liked each other, even if they sounded like they were teasing. "If you let me use your wire, I'll make a motorcycle," Rohan said, after he was done trying to kick rocks onto Ella's shoes.

"Okay, I'm going to teach Shanna this weekend, but we might be going to her house, so you can't come over," Ella said. "We're going to color eggs and that really is a girl thing."

"It is not a girl thing," Rye said as he swung around one of the swing-set poles. The little kids had been outside even before the fifth graders.

"Shanna, when are we going to color eggs?"

"Don't sneak up on me, Rye!" Shanna squeaked. "And Momma said we'll do it on Saturday. I'm going to ask if Ella can come, because she's never done it before."

"I'll color eggs," Rohan said. "Can I come too? I don't think Ella knows what boy things and girl things are."

"I know!" Ella yelled but she was still giggling.

Shanna was going to say that she would ask Momma if Rohan could come too, but then Brandy and her friends, including Rebecca, stepped up behind the swings, and the words stuck in Shanna's tight throat.

"You're going to hell," Brandy said, her fists on her hips as she looked at Shanna. "My dad says your necklace really is a devil worshipper necklace and you're a Satanist. You're gonna burn in a big fire with all the bad people."

Rye's eyes were round with shock and Ella's mouth made a little O. Everyone else was quiet, waiting to see what Shanna would say. Shanna just stared back. She didn't know what a "Satanist" or a "devil-worshipper" was.

"Show her how dirty she is," one of the other girls yelled.

She took her hands out from behind her back and ran right at Shanna. Her hands were covered with thick mud from the edge of the playground. Two other girls followed and they all shrieked with laughter, smearing the mud on Shanna's coat and pants. Brandy laughed too, but she kept her hands in her pockets.

"Stop it!" Ella screamed. And Rye grabbed the jacket of one girl, trying to pull her away from Shanna.

"Oh, shut up, Ella," Brandy said. "You're not a real Christian either and you'll end up in hell too."

Shanna slid off the swing and tried to back away, but the girls were all around her blocking her and grabbing at her coat. Her legs felt wobbly and when someone grabbed her from behind, Shanna stumbled and fell to her knees in the mud.

She was scared but it also felt unreal, like a dream or something on TV. Then someone yanked at the back of her shirt and Shanna felt cold, gritty gravel on her skin—all too real. The girls shrieked and the gravel tumbled down inside Shanna's shirt and stuck in the waistband of her pants.

Shanna tried to squirm away from them. Her fists were clenched and she had something in one of her palms. She had taken her hands out of her pockets and she was clinging hard to Skylar's pendant, so that the raised image of the vine cut into her fingers.

"Yuck! She has that thing!" one of the girls shrieked.

"Oooo! You want to put a spell on us, witch!" Brandy taunted as the girls broke away and started to run.

But then a stern voice interrupted. "What is going on here, girls?" Mrs. Baker was half running toward them with Rohan towing her by her sleeve. The teacher's face was turning red and her eyes narrowed. "Fighting is a serious offense."

"She was after us with that Satanic thing that you told her not to bring to school!" Brandy yelled.

Tears seemed to fill Shanna's throat. She couldn't speak and she knew that they would laugh if she cried. She bit her lip so hard that she tasted blood and she shook her head.

"Let me see," Mrs. Baker demanded,

holding her hand out.

Her eyes were suspicious and Shanna felt like something was squeezing her chest. She held onto the pendant in her hand as tightly as she could.

"It's my necklace from my friend," she managed to say without crying. "I didn't wear it. It was in my pocket."

"Let me see it!" Mrs. Baker barked and snapped her fingers.

Shanna didn't want to give her Skylar's gift, but she knew she could get in really big trouble if she didn't listen to a teacher. So she held the necklace up and put it in Mrs. Baker's outstretched hand.

"Please…" she said but she couldn't say more and her hands shook.

Mrs. Baker glared at the pendant and then took the leather thong between the thumb and forefinger of her other hand and held it up so that the pentacle dangled. Her face was all screwed up and her eyes narrowed as if she was holding a dead mouse.

"Shanna Silver, you need to come with me to the office," she said.

"But Mrs. Baker, they were after her! Shanna didn't do anything!" Ella cried.

"I didn't see anyone chasing her," Mrs. Baker said. "What I see is that she has been rolling around in the mud fighting and she brought this thing back to school when I told her expressly that it wasn't allowed."

The teacher turned back to Shanna and snapped, "Get a move on."

Rohan glared and clenched his fist.

Shanna walked toward the school building with her

head down. Bits of gravel fell out of the bottom of her coat and she could hear Brandy and the other girls laughing and singing, "Ella's going to hell! Shanna's going to hell!" under their breath.

Rye ran to catch up with Shanna and tugged at her sleeve. He had tears on his cheeks.

"Shanna, why do you have to go to the office? Why?"

"Dear," Mrs. Baker said sternly. "You need to go back to your class. Shanna is going to the office because she was fighting."

Mrs. Baker walked behind Shanna, but she loomed so large over her that Shanna felt like running. She fought her tears back again. Mrs. Baker would probably take away the necklace and Shanna would never get it back. She missed Skylar and Mrs. Durrett and everyone at her old school so much that her heart hurt in her chest.

Rye was left outside. Mrs. Baker nudged Shanna into the office and then past the front desk. Shanna had already been in the front office when they came to register, but now the big, dark brown door of the principal's office opened and she had to go in.

Her knees were trembling so hard that they knocked together. She clenched her fists and swallowed hard.

Mrs. Taylor, the principal, had been nice when they met

her with Momma, but Shanna hadn't seen her since. She was older than Momma and she had caramel-colored skin. Shanna was surprised that even a few days ago, she had thought darker skin was strange, but now she was used to all the different shades. Mrs. Taylor smiled at Shanna, but then she turned sober as she listened to the teacher's complaint.

Mrs. Baker held out Shanna's pentacle necklace and told the principal that Shanna was "showing off this thing" and "picking fights." Mrs. Taylor took the necklace from Mrs. Baker and pursed her lips as she laid it on her desk.

"I would say that could be considered a gang symbol," Mrs. Baker said.

"Well, if it's disruptive, that's the main issue," Mrs. Taylor said. "I'll call her mother and we'll have a talk about it."

"She comes in here and immediately starts with this,"

Mrs. Baker said. Her face was still red, but Mrs. Taylor repeated that she would handle it and Mrs. Baker left.

Once the door was closed Mrs. Taylor looked at Shanna and she had a little crease between her eyebrows.

"Shanna, would you like to tell me what this is?" she asked, pointing at the pendant on her desk.

"It isn't true," Shanna said. Now her voice was shaking and tears were starting to come out of her eyes, no matter how hard she tried to hold them back. "I wasn't fighting. They put mud on me and I was just holding my necklace. I didn't mean to. It was supposed to be in my pocket."

"Hush!" Mrs. Taylor said sternly. Her face wasn't angry though, just firm. "I only asked you what this is."

Shanna gulped back her crying and took a deep breath, filling her belly with air the way Momma had taught her. She wiped her eyes quickly with her sleeve and then looked back up at Mrs. Taylor and spoke as calmly as she could.

"That's a necklace that my friend gave me," Shanna said.

"What friend?" Mrs. Taylor asked.

"My best friend from my old school," Shanna said. "She has one just like it. It's my friendship necklace."

"And do you know what is on it?" Mrs. Taylor asked.

"Yes, it's a pentacle," Shanna said. "And a vine."

Mrs. Taylor nodded slowly as if that was very important. "Well, do you know what it means?"

Shanna stopped. It was hard to remember. She knew Momma had a pentacle on her altar and some of the Tarot cards had pentacles on them. And once she thought Momma had told her. She tried to remember.

"Each point stands for something," she said

uncertainly. "Water, air, earth, fire and spirit, I think."

Mrs. Taylor blinked as if she was surprised by this. Then she reached over to the big phone on her desk and picked it up. She punched a button and spoke into the  receiver, asking someone to call Shanna's mom. Then she waited a minute, still watching Shanna.

In a minute, Shanna thought she could hear Momma's voice, tiny and far away on the phone. The principal talked for a moment, saying that Shanna had been in a fight at school and there was trouble about "some disruptive jewelry." Then Mrs. Taylor listened and said, "Yes," and "I understand," a few times.

Finally she hung up.

"Your mother says she'll come this afternoon to discuss this," Mrs. Taylor said. "You can go back to class, Shanna, but I'm going to keep the necklace for now and I want you to know that this is your only warning about fighting. If you are involved with fighting again, there will be serious consequences."

Chapter Four

Keeping the Balance

Shanna walked slowly back to Mrs. Baker's class. Recess was over. She stopped at the bathroom and wiped at the mud on her pants and coat. She also dug the last few pieces of gravel out of the waistband of her pants.

Tears streamed down her cheeks now that she was alone. She didn't make any noise, but she let the tears fall down so that they would all be gone when she went back to class. She didn't want to give Brandy and the other girls the satisfaction of seeing how sad they'd made her.

She washed her face and then went back to the classroom.

When she opened the door, Mrs. Baker stopped talking at the front of the room and said, "Come in, Shanna, and have a seat."

Brandy and a bunch of the other kids snickered quietly as Shanna walked to her seat. Ella's face looked sad and even Rebecca looked serious. She wasn't laughing with the others.

Rebecca had been with the girls who smeared mud on Shanna but she had only watched.

Shanna slid into her place and looked at her hands on her desk, and Mrs. Baker continued with the lesson.

When the lunch bell rang, Rohan jumped out of his seat and came quickly over to Shanna.

"I'm really, really sorry!" he whispered, while all the other kids were getting up. "I ran to get Mrs. Baker because I thought she'd help you. It's not fair that you got in trouble."

Ella came up on the other side of Shanna and touched her hair. "What happened?" she asked sympathetically.

Shanna told them about the principal in a low voice while they walked to lunch and then the three of them sat together at a table.

"Yeah, you have to keep things like that out of sight," Rohan said. He fished at his own shirt collar and pulled something out with a gold chain. He held it cupped between his hands so that no one else could see. Shanna and Ella both gasped in amazement.

It was a little golden monkey… or sort of a monkey and sort of a person with a tail. The figure was kneeling with its hands raised as if it was praying or possibly ready to make a Karate chop.

"What's that?" Shanna asked.

"Hanuman," Rohan said. "It's real gold too. Don't tell anyone."

31

He stuffed it quickly back into his shirt.

"My dad doesn't want me to show everyone because someone might steal it," he said. "But I don't think it would be a good idea to show it anyway."

"You're not Christian either," Ella said and she sounded amazed and a little shocked.

"Nope," Rohan laughed. "I'm Hindu."

"Well, I am a Christian, no matter what those girls say," Ella sniffed.

"You're Catholic, right?" Rohan asked.

Ella nodded.

"Yeah, some people think anyone who isn't the exact same as them is bad," he said. "Are we still friends, even if I'm not going to become a Christian?"

Ella giggled. "Of course, we're friends, you dummie."

"Good. Just checking," Rohan said. Then he turned to Shanna. "So what are you?"

Shanna's mouth was already open while she watched their discussion. Now she just stared at Rohan for a second.

Then she said, "I'm... I'm just me."

"I mean, what church or temple do you go to and what was that star thingie?" he asked.

"It's a pentacle. And... well, we don't go to church. We have our own gods and the earth and..."

Shanna stopped. She realized that she had heard words that she could use. Momma had never said, "You have to be this," or "We are that." But she had talked about different groups, when they had gone to the big gatherings and community rituals last year.

"I think we're called Pagan," she said.

Ella's eyes widened and her mouth made an O again.

But Rohan shrugged.

"I haven't heard of that," he said. "So, you have more than one god?"

"Yeah," Shanna said. "And the earth is really important to us."

"That's good," Rohan said.

Ella still looked startled but she nodded. "I think that's okay too," she said at last.

Momma came before school was out. She knocked on the classroom door while they were finishing up their history collages and stood in the doorway. Mrs. Baker told Shanna to go, so she jumped up and got her things.

Out in the hallway, Momma gave Shanna a hug and looked into her face carefully. Shanna told her what had happened. And she could tell right away that she wasn't going to get in trouble with Momma. Instead Momma took Shanna's hand firmly the way she had when Shanna was a little girl. Then they went down to the lower floor to get Rye.

"Are we going home?" Shanna asked.

"In a little bit," Momma said. "For now we're going to talk to the principal."

Rye looked sad when he came out of his classroom.

"Are you okay, honey?" Momma asked him.

"Yeah, but I don't like this school," Rye mumbled. Then he spoke more clearly but still quietly. "The kids are mean. They call me a 'girlie' because I like to draw and because I said I'd sing in the spring play we're doing. The teacher asked for anyone who wanted to sing and I like to sing. But they said boys can't sing, only girls."

"What does the teacher say?" Momma bent her knees

so that she could look Rye right in the eyes.

"She said I'm brave because I was the only boy who would sing," he said. "And she made Lars apologize."

Momma gave a little sigh and hugged Rye.

"Well, she's right about that. You are super brave. Boys certainly can sing and draw just as well as girls. Look at all the famous singers who are men and boys. They can make a million dollars. You think about that a minute."

Then they walked to the principal's office. When they were standing in the front office, the secretary told Momma the kids should wait on the couch across from her desk.

But Momma said, "No thank you, Mrs. Dixon. I want my children to learn about conflict resolution."

Then she knocked on Mrs. Taylor's door.

Mrs. Taylor stood up and shook Momma's hand, saying she was sorry to have to call her in and that it's sometimes hard for kids to learn about getting along.

Momma smiled pleasantly and sat down in a chair, motioning for Shanna and Rye to sit too.

Mrs. Taylor gave them a puzzled frown, but then Momma said, "I think we need to have a serious discussion with the children."

"Yes, I'm told Shanna was involved with a fight today and I want you to know we have a zero-tolerance policy for that kind of behavior," Mrs. Taylor said.

"If that's the case." Momma cleared her throat with a cough. "I would like to know what kind of mediation is planned with the students who attacked Shanna."

"I have no report that she was attacked." Mrs. Taylor's tone was sharp all of the sudden.

"Shanna, please stand up." Momma nodded at Shanna. "And turn around, honey."

Shanna stood and slowly turned in a circle, even though she didn't know why Momma wanted her to.

"Do you see the smudges on her coat from mud?" Momma asked.

"Yes," Mrs. Taylor said. "I was told she was rolling around on the ground fighting with another girl."

"That is what you were told, but the playground dirt doesn't make smudges with five fingers visible when you roll on the ground, does it?' Momma said.

The principal beckoned for Shanna to come nearer and

then she half rose out of her chair to peer at Shanna's coat and at the legs of her pants.

"Well, I am sorry, Shanna," she said finally. "I should have looked at this before."

Shanna felt her heart start to beat stronger inside and she smiled at Momma.

"Now, about the necklace," Momma said.

"Yes." Mrs. Taylor nodded at Momma. "I'll admit that the fight might not be the way I was told, but the teacher has made more than one complaint already about Shanna showing this necklace off and it's disruptive. In fact, it might be considered a gang symbol. That sort of thing can lead to trouble even if Shanna didn't intend to fight."

Mrs. Taylor held up the pentacle by its thong and displayed it before Momma. "Do you recognize this, Mrs. Silver?"

"I sure do," Momma said. "That's my daughter's necklace, which was given to her by a friend."

"I'm afraid your daughter may have some friends who aren't the best influences." Mrs. Taylor said. "Do you know what the symbol means?"

Momma smiled calmly. "I certainly do know what the pentacle means. It's a symbol of our beliefs and my daughter has my full support in wearing it. It's a symbol of balance and harmony."

Mrs. Taylor's face looked flat and startled for a minute. "I've been told that it's a symbol for a certain subculture among teens," she said a bit more hesitantly.

"I can't speak for every group that may have adopted a five-pointed star as a symbol," Momma said. "But this isn't a gang symbol and it's a recognized religious symbol for earth-centered and Pagan faiths."

Mrs. Taylor held out the pentacle to Shanna. "All right, Mrs. Silver," she said. "Have it your way. That's your private affair. I'll simply ask that Shanna doesn't bring it to school anymore because it is disruptive and we'll leave it at that."

Chapter Five

Celebration

As Shanna, Rye and Momma walked out of the principal's office, the bell rang. Shanna squeezed Momma's hand and asked if Ella and Rohan could come over the next day to color eggs.

"That's a wonderful idea, Shanna," Momma said with an encouraging smile.

Shanna hurried up the hall to tell Rohan and Ella.

When they got home the sun was shining and violets and tiny buttercups were peeking up through the matted dead grass in the yard. By the steps to the porch there were long bright green shoots with something bulging at the ends. Shanna finally felt like Ostara was really coming.

Momma and Rye started getting out decorations and materials. They were going to make natural egg dyes by boiling onion skins, beets, purple cabbage and turmeric powder, so they would be ready in the morning.

Shanna kept her jacket on and sat on the back step to

start on her homework and look over the chapters Mrs. Baker had suggested. She tried not to think about how unfair her new teacher was. The sweet-smelling breeze and the warm sunlight gave her plenty of energy. She decided she would get all of her homework done the first night, so she'd have the

whole weekend to play and have a joyful Ostara, no matter what anyone else said.

She held her lip between her teeth and bent over the math problems until her head buzzed. Then she got up and did jumping jacks while she practiced the spelling list.

By the time the sun was going down and birds were twittering and hopping about in the backyard trees, Shanna was done with everything except reading for science. And that was hardly homework because she loved science. She'd read it before bed.

The next morning Rohan and Ella came at ten o'clock. Momma had eggs and crayons ready for them and pans of dye on the stove.

"I thought you use colored paint on the eggs," Ella said when she saw the crayons. "This won't make very nice pictures."

"Just you wait and see." Shanna gave her a mysterious smile and took a bowl of warm wax from the kitchen. "You make pictures on the eggs with crayons or hot wax and then you dye them. And the pictures show up white under the color. It's the best!"

Rohan sat down by Rye and started carefully putting dots of wax onto an egg with a toothpick. Shanna made hearts, stars, pentacles and moon shapes all over her eggs. Then she showed Rohan and Ella how to dunk them in the various colored dyes.

There was dark, dusky red from the peels of red onions, rich golden brown from brown onions, pink from beets, blue from purple cabbage and yellow from tumeric. You could even make the eggs have more than two colors by dying them

a light color like pink or yellow, adding more wax pictures over the color and then putting them into a darker color. Momma had one pot where she had left the onion peels in the dye instead of straining them out and the eggs she put in there came out all covered with swirls and patterns from the onion peels.

"I saw the egg colors they have in the store," Rohan said. "You don't have to boil onions and stuff to make them."

"Yes, that's true," Momma said. "But the colors get inside the eggs and they aren't very good to eat after that. It's important not to waste the gifts of the earth, so we're going to eat our eggs when we're done with them. Our dyes make the eggs taste even better and they won't give you headaches and jitters like the synthetic colors do."

When the eggs were all colored, Momma got out bread, cheese and some greens from the garden and let everyone decorate their own sandwiches. They got to add slices of boiled egg from the eggs that had accidentally cracked while they were coloring them.

"Can I ask something?" Ella said timidly when Momma had left the room.

Shanna was surprised. Ella was usually a chatterbox and she'd ask anything even if no one knew the answer.

"What?" Shanna said.

"Well, why do you color Easter eggs, if you aren't Christians?" Ella asked.

Rye stared at Ella and Rohan glared at her like he wanted her to shut up.

"They aren't Easter eggs. They're Ostara eggs," Rye said. He winked at Shanna and giggles bubbled up inside her.

"We call it Ostara but it's a lot like Easter, even though Ostara comes first," Shanna explained. "My mom says Easter comes from the word Ostara too. Ostara is a goddess who brings spring and helps make baby animals and baby people and baby plants. She loves eggs and flowers. That's why we decorate with those things in the spring."

"And her best friend is a rabbit…" Rye put in. " Well, actually a hare. And that's why you've got an Ostara bunny or an Easter bunny."

Rohan laughed too and took a big bite of his sandwich. "I think they've got you there Ella. How come you paint eggs when you're not a Pagan and you don't even have goddesses?"

"Oh, stop talking with your mouth full!" Ella giggled and threw a napkin at him.

When Momma came back in from the kitchen, she poured them all some fresh lemonade and asked if they wanted to make Ostara cookies. So, they rolled out the dough and used rabbit—or hare, as Rye insisted they were—cookie cutters to make sugar cookies. And while they baked Ella showed them how to make little baskets for individual eggs with her craft wires.

All in all it was a perfect day. When the others went home for dinner, Shanna realized she hadn't missed her old school and her old friends all day long.

Early the next morning, they got up before the sun and lit candles on the new altar in the living room. There were little egg cups full of sprouting grass set around the edges and Rye brought stuffed animals that looked like babies—a duckling, a baby mouse and a baby penguin.

Momma asked them to stand with their feet planted firmly and they each held one of the drums they kept near the altar. Momma began a slow beat and Shanna and Rye echoed the soft rhythm like winter snow.

"Your heart is filled with light. Your arms and your legs

are filled with light," Momma said in rhythm with the drum. "From your feet roots go down into the floor. Down. Down. Down. And into the foundation of the house. Down Down. Down. And into the earth."

Shanna imagined big gnarled tree roots coming out of the bottoms of her feet and going into the earth, rooting her deep and strong. Gradually the drum beat sped up. Shanna struck her drum a little harder and a little harder until all three drums boomed inside the living room.

Shanna and Rye whooped and laughed and sang with the beat while the sun came over the horizon and spilled golden light into the living room.

After the circle was finished it was time to go outside and search for their decorated eggs and a few chocolate ones that the hare of Ostara had hidden for them all over the backyard. Shanna and Rye ran for their coats and they each got a basket with dried grass in the bottom of it.

"Be careful not to step on the new flowers," Momma

chuckled as they ran out the back door. "We want to make sure the fairies live in our new garden."

The two fruit trees in the yard—one apple and one plum—didn't have blossoms yet but the whole yard smelled wonderful with fresh soil and early morning dew. Shanna and Rye found little pathways between the shrubs and trees while they searched for the eggs. Some of the eggs were just propped in the branches of the trees or set on top of overturned flower pots. But some were really well hidden under new leaves and disguised by the bright purple and sparkling yellow of the violets.

They found two birds nests while they were searching but they were careful not to touch them, so that the birds would come back.

When they couldn't find any more eggs, they each picked out one perfect and beautiful egg from their baskets. These they carried to a big boulder at the end of the garden and left them on top of it—for the fairies and the hare, in case he came back.

Then they ran back in the house to Momma, who was making a big breakfast of omelets and raisin scones with honey.

"This is a special Ostara for us," Momma said when they were mostly finished eating and the sun in the window was warming Shanna's back and shoulders. "We are really starting something new here and I know it isn't easy for you, so I have a little present for each of you."

She held out two little packages.

Shanna slowly pulled the thin tissue paper away from her package and then she smiled. There was a little pack of cards with beautiful black and white drawings on each one and a packet of thick, wooden colored pencils—the good kind that don't break.

"Thanks, Momma!" Rye said. He held up his own pack of colored pencils and a coloring book. His coloring book said "Gods, Goddesses and Heroes" on it and had a picture of a woman with long skirts and a sword on the front.

"I know you wanted that book when we saw it at the store, Rye,"

Momma said. "That's a special grown-up drawing book, but I think you're big enough for it."

"I'll be careful with it," Rye said.

"It shows you how to draw people and it also tells you about some warrior goddesses and brave heroes too," Momma added.

"So, it will help you remember to keep every part of you strong--the parts that are like goddesses and the parts that are like gods too."

Shanna peered at her own cards and realized that they looked like Momma's Tarot deck, except they had no color.

"These will be your first Tarot deck," Momma said gently. "You can color them in whatever way feels right to you. Your heart will tell you the best way and then your energy will be strong in the cards. And you will start to learn how to use them as your allies and helpers. I know it's especially hard for you to start again in this new school and you might need some extra friends."

"Thanks," Shanna smiled and leaned over to hug Momma. She pressed the deck of special cards to her chest and felt her own heart beating, strong and quick.

Chapter Six

Opening the Door

On Monday, the classroom was finally full of egg, bunny and flower decorations, even though Ostara had already passed. Mrs. Baker asked for volunteers to read poems or verses at the Easter program. Brandy and several other girls raised their hands.

Mrs. Baker also said they would do two art projects for Easter that week. Shanna listened silently. She had always liked school art projects and at her old school, she had never minded the projects that focused on other people's holidays. But her old teacher had also had spring projects and she hadn't cared what sort of necklaces the kids wore.

Now Shanna had a hard ball of anger and frustration in her stomach. She was angry at Mrs. Baker, but she was also a little angry at Momma.

Why couldn't Momma just celebrate the same holidays as everyone else? If she did, then Shanna wouldn't have any of these problems.

At recess, Shanna went outside with Rohan and Ella. Rohan said he was taking a day off of school for Holi on Wednesday.

"That's like Easter too, sort of," he said. "It's about having fun and making bright colors. And kids get money. It's really cool when you go to a big party where everyone throws colored water in the air and your clothes are all crazy rainbows."

Shanna smiled. It did sound like fun.

"I don't think my mom would let me get rainbow paint all over my new Easter dress," Ella laughed.

A spatter of muddy water rained across them and Ella and Shanna spun around to see Brandy and the other girls walking away giggling.

"You're going to burn!" one of the girls yelled over her shoulder.

Rebecca stood watching a few feet away. She was wearing a cross on a necklace too. It was ivory white and it stood out brightly against her neck.

Rebecca saw Shanna looking at her and she turned away.

Shanna heard yelling from the top of the slide and several boys tumbled down the slope at once. Her heart jumped when she recognized Rye's coat amid the mass of arms and legs. He landed on his back in the mud at the bottom of the slide and he was clutching something to his chest.

Two boys were grabbing him from either side and trying to tear whatever it was out of his hands. Rye ducked low and charged under their hands, away from the slide and toward the swings.

She started toward them with her fists clenched, hot anger boiling in her belly.

"No, Shanna!" Rohan grabbed her arm. "Tell the teacher! If you fight them, you'll really get in trouble."

"You saw what happened last time," Shanna shot back. "The teachers aren't going to help."

Rye jumped onto a swing and held the coloring book in his hand high off the ground. Then he started pumping his feet and the swing careened wildly back and forth so that the other boys had to stay back.

"I don't care what you say!" Rye called out. Shanna stared. He wasn't even crying. Instead he was laughing. "I'm going to draw if I want to. And sing!"

He was moving faster now on the swing and he started to sing the theme song to Iron Man, while the other boys stood back. One of the teachers came across the playground and gave the boys surrounding the swing a long, hard look. They dropped their heads and walked away.

Shanna let out a sigh and loosened her clenched fists.

That afternoon they played basketball in P.E. Mrs. Baker made everyone take off their necklaces for that. Shanna noticed that all of Brandy's friends were wearing crosses this time. Only Rebecca had worn one before, but now that Shanna couldn't wear her pentacle necklace it had become a new fad.

Mrs. Baker made a little speech before they played.

"I've been noticing some squabbles among you these past few days," she said. "I want everyone to remember how to be friends, so I'm going to start breaking you up into different groups."

That meant that Shanna and Ella weren't on the same

team. Instead Shanna was on a team with Brandy, Rebecca and a few of the other mean girls.

Brandy stepped on Shanna's foot on purpose twice during the game and some of the others elbowed her hard when they could tell Mrs. Baker wasn't looking. By the end of the game, Shanna felt sore and grumpy.

Shanna's team lost, so they had to put the balls back. It was the last hour of the day, and everyone else could get changed and go home.

"Brandy, I expect you to be a good friendliness ambassador and show Shanna where to put the balls," Mrs. Baker called after them. "Shanna, I'll see you in the office when you're done. Your mom is coming to talk with Mrs. Taylor and me."

Shanna felt a sharp stab of worry run up her legs. Momma hadn't said anything about this. Was she in trouble again because of the way she had been angry at those boys? Shanna hadn't actually done anything.

It wasn't fair!

Brandy and the others laughed. "Shanna's in trouble!" they chanted softly as they each scooped up a ball, leaving Shanna to try to carry three at once.

"This is where the balls go, witch," Brandy said, as they approached a scratched, blue door in the back corner of the gym. Brandy had to slide a bar out of an old-fashioned latch to get it open. And once it was open, several volleyballs rolled out into the hallway.

"You better put all the balls back in their bins," Brandy said, giving Shanna a push into the dark storage room. "Otherwise, I'll tell Mrs. Baker you wouldn't help us… like a Christian would."

Shanna stumbled over the volleyballs and fell down hard with the basket balls going every which way. Then all of the sudden the door slammed behind her, cutting off the light from the hallway.

Shanna gave a little shriek. She was startled and even a little afraid.

She could hear wild laughing and the metal latch being pushed back into place. She jumped up and ran toward the sound. She hit the door, but she was too late. It only rattled and otherwise didn't budge.

"Let me out!" she screamed.

The girls on the other side screeched in gales of laughter. "You might as well get used to it!" Brandy yelled. "Hell is dark like that. That's where you're going!"

There were more shrieks and giggles and then the sound of their feet on the gym floor as they ran away.

"Help! Let me out!" Shanna screamed as loud as she could and banged on the door. The darkness was all around her inside the ball closet and she felt the balls tap against her legs like something alive.

She started shaking and tears welled up in her eyes. "Let me out! Don't leave me here!" she hiccuped more softly.

But they were gone. There was only silence outside and all Shanna could see was a thin line of light at the bottom of the door. She gulped back her sobs.

She remembered that darkness is not bad. The earth is dark. The night sky with the moon and stars is dark. Shanna reminded herself that both of those are the homes of mother goddesses who protect children and heal people when they're sick. Darkness is comforting when it's time to sleep at night.

Shanna stood still for a moment and made the image in

her mind of tree roots going down from the soles of her feet into the floor and through it into the foundation of the school and then into the earth below. Her trembling calmed and her breath came more slowly.

Then Shanna opened her eyes and started feeling around the edge of the door for a light switch. After a minute she found it and a square light on the ceiling flickered on.

The closet wasn't so scary after all. It just had a ball net, some pads and big wire baskets on huge shelves at the back.

Shanna started tossing the basketballs and the loose volley balls into the bins where they belonged. Then she heard footsteps outside the door.

"Hey, who's there? I'm stuck in here. Please let me out!" Shanna called and she knocked on the door with her knuckles.

The bar outside lifted and the door cracked open.

Shanna stared in amazement. Rebecca peered

in around the door. Her hair stuck out in pretty braids with beads woven in them, but she looked serious and worried.

"Are you okay, Shanna?" she asked and she swung the door all the way open. "I'm sorry. We've been mean to you, but I'm not like that. I don't want to be."

Shanna felt her knees shivering a little bit, but she was very happy to see Rebecca and to have the door open.

"Yeah, I'm okay," Shanna said slowly and she came out of the closet, just to make sure Rebecca wouldn't change her mind and shut her back inside.

"I'm really sorry," Rebecca said again. "I'll go with you to the office and I'll tell the principal that you weren't fighting last week, if you want."

Shanna stared at her, amazed. "Thanks," she said.

Chapter Seven

Both Gentle and Strong

The two of them walked through the empty gym and into the hallway. Almost everyone else was already outside and Shanna shivered, thinking about how long she might have been locked in the gym closet if Rebecca hadn't come back for her.

"Brandy will be mad that you let me out," Shanna told Rebecca, as they came out into the big hall by the principal's office.

"I don't care," Rebecca said. "I'd rather have Brandy mad at me than have God mad at me." She bit her lip. "And the principal."

"I won't tell the principal," Shanna said. "And I don't think gods get mad at us. They help us and give us things to learn—like it doesn't matter what color or religion my friends are."

They walked into the front office together and the secretary looked up. "Shanna, your mom's here. Mrs. Taylor said you can go right in. Rebecca dear, do you need something?"

"She's coming with me," Shanna said.

The secretary blinked at them behind her glasses and shrugged. "We'll see what Mrs. Taylor has to say."

Shanna knocked at the big shiny door to Mrs. Taylor's office and someone opened it from inside.

Momma was there, sitting in one of the chairs with Rye on her knee and Mrs. Baker and another teacher were there too.

"What?" Mrs. Baker said. "What's Rebecca doing here?"

"She wanted to come with me and I said she could," Shanna said, glancing at Mrs. Taylor.

"I'd say that's actually a good idea," Mrs. Taylor said from behind her desk.

She motioned for Rebecca and Shanna to sit on a couple of folding chairs that had been set up in the office and then she continued, "Girls, we are having a meeting about some of the problems in your classroom. It's my job to make sure this school is a safe place for everyone. First, each of us is going to say how we feel and what we want to happen. And everyone else will listen without interrupting, okay?"

Shanna and Rebecca nodded. Shanna still felt scared but Mrs. Taylor didn't look mad. In fact, her eyes were steady and calm.

"I feel like I'm being backed into a corner here!" Mrs. Baker said. "I just don't want disruptive stuff and symbols of violence and Satanism in my classroom. I've read about it and a lot of Christians believe this is a Satanic symbol used to hurt children. I want all this hysteria over a necklace to stop."

Mrs. Taylor nodded and smiled at Momma.

"I feel worried about my children being safe here and I want them to be able to wear symbols of our faith if they want to," Momma said.

The lines of many smiles in her face made her look  strong and her voice was kind but very firm, like when she told Shanna and Rye to do their chores.

"The pentacle isn't a symbol of violence," Momma explained. "It's a recognized religious symbol for earth-centered faiths. I have a list of school board decisions on the subject. Even our soldiers serving in the military recognize the pentacle as our religious symbol and place it on official grave stones. We are not Satanists and we don't promote violence. If my children cannot wear their symbols, then I want the school to ban all religious symbols, including necklaces with crosses. If it is that important to you, you should be willing to make a small sacrifice."

Mrs. Taylor nodded gently, even though Mrs. Baker was breathing loud and glaring at Momma.

"Shanna, could you tell us how you feel about this?" Mrs. Taylor asked.

Shanna swallowed and looked down at her hands for a second. Then she took a deep breath and looked directly into

Mrs. Taylor's eyes, even though it made her stomach twist with worry.

"I feel scared because some kids have been saying mean things and throwing mud on me," she said. "I'm sad because I can't wear my necklace. I'm new here and my necklace is from my friend. It makes me feel better to wear it. I want to be friends with the other kids and I want to be able to say that we have Ostara instead of Easter without getting in trouble."

Then Mrs. Taylor looked at Rebecca. "You aren't in trouble, Rebecca, but you can say how you feel if you want to," she said.

"I... I..." Rebecca stammered a little but then she also took a deep breath. "I feel scared sometimes too. I'm scared that I have to say things I don't like in order to have friends. I want to be friends with everyone. And I would be sad if I couldn't wear my cross to school because my grandma gave it to me before she died and it's really important to me."

Shanna felt how scared Rebecca was because Rebecca was shivering on the chair right next to her. So, Shanna put her hand on Rebecca's hand and gave it a little squeeze.

Rebecca looked at her and smiled.

Mrs. Taylor sighed very deep and sat back with her fingers folded on her desk. "We can have a big argument about this and take it to the school board if we have to," she said. "But I think I know how that would turn out. Mrs. Silver is correct that there have been several school boards faced with this issue and the decision has almost always gone in favor of allowing the use of these religious symbols. I'll admit that I always thought this pentacle was a symbol of Satanists, but after reading about it, I see that it's different. I would like to offer a compromise because Mrs. Baker and others are worried about this being used as a gang symbol. Students can wear the pentacle symbol if they correctly identify it as a religious symbol and know what it means. This would ensure that we can all continue to wear our religious symbols."

Mrs. Taylor's hand strayed to the collar of her shirt and she turned it back to show a thin silver chain with a very small cross hanging on it.

There was a long moment of silence and when no one else seemed ready to speak Shanna said, "I know what the pentacle means. It's about all the life that comes from the earth. And that's what Ostara is about too. It's about babies being born and seeds sprouting and kids running and playing and having fun. It's not about anything bad. There's a circle around it like everyone holding hands and being friends."

Rebecca grinned at her and squeezed Shanna's hand back.

"I think that says it pretty well indeed," Momma said, letting out her breath with a little laugh.

Mrs. Baker looked less angry now. "That was nicely said, Shanna," she said. "And I appreciate how you are making friends with Rebecca. I have to admit that I don't like that pentacle, but what is in your heart is most important. I can respect Mrs. Taylor's compromise."

Shanna and Rebecca walked out of the school together. Rebecca's mom was waiting for her and tapping her foot impatiently.

"Where have you been? I hope you haven't been in trouble again, Becca!" she burst out when she saw them.

"Not at all," Momma said. "I'm Tamie Silver and this is my daughter Shanna and my son Rye. We're new here and Rebecca was helping us work something out. She's very grown up."

Rebecca's mom looked relieved and she tugged playfully at one of Rebecca's braids.

Rebecca gave a gasp and pointed at the tree they were passing near the swing set. A bird fluttered into it, covering the bright blue peeking out from the soft hollow.

"There are eggs in our school nest!" Shanna burst out.

They all peered at the nest from a distance and Shanna waved to Rebecca as they walked toward Momma's car.

"Yay! We won!" Rye gave a little whoop.

"Rye, honey," Momma said. "Not everything is a fight. Sometimes people are just scared of things they don't know. Sometimes they've been told things that aren't true. When people learn to be friends, then everybody wins."

She opened the car door and Shanna went around to the other side to get in.

As they drove out of the parking lot, Shanna said, "I'm glad if I can wear the necklace from Skylar again and I'm glad Rebecca will be my friend."

"We're lucky that the law is on our side," Momma said. "There have been many times when Pagans and lots of other people have not been able to openly show their beliefs. At another time, it might have been different, even dangerous. Sometimes even when the law is on your side it's safer to keep your beliefs in your own heart. This is one of the times when it is okay to say what you think, but we have to be strong and peaceful and remember to listen to other people too. The only way we will be respected is if we show what we believe by our actions."

Shanna got out of the car at home and gasped in delight when she saw the front yard that was now covered with buttercups and violets peeking out of last year's matted grass. By the porch steps, the bulges on top of the green shoots had burst and each one was now topped with a white flower that had a golden cup in the center.

"Oh, Momma!" Shanna shouted. "They're so beautiful!"

"I thought you'd like them," Momma said. "Those are narcissus paperwhites. Someone before us planted them here. They have bulbs that stay safe under the ground when it's cold out and they come up again each spring."

"I guess they know how to show themselves when the right time comes," Shanna laughed and gave Momma a hug. The smell of the narcissus was sweet and fresh, like something a goddess might wear.

"Yes, they do," Momma said. "Now is a good time for a new beginning. Like those flowers pushing up through the hard cold dirt, we can be gentle and strong at the same time, can't we?"

"Sure we can!" Rye said. And he took out his coloring book and sat down on the grass amid the flowers.

The Children's Wheel of the Year

The Children's Wheel of the Year is a series of books for earth-centered families. The next story will center on Beltane and the things that arouse our passions, including the protecting the earth.

This year Shanna and Rye can't go to a big Beltane festival. Instead they invite friends and put up a maypole on a hill behind the school. The hill—with wild grass and scrubby trees--is called "wasted land" by some. In school, Shanna's teacher talks about a "water crisis" and how the land is too dry. Later they take a field trip to the hill because the teacher says it will soon be leveled and covered with buildings..

They crawl through the brush and climb on rocks until Shanna finds a little pool made by water trickling out of an outcrop under some big trees. Soon the kids realize this spring feeds a whole line of green down into town. But the teacher says the spring will die if the trees are cut and the area is bulldozed. Shanna and her friends decide they have to do something to save the spring.

Children in earth-centered families hear a lot about environmental problems and harm to the earth. It can be overwhelming and we often feel hopeless. This is a story of hope, passion and strength, based on a real incident of what happens when kids take action.

**The next story is
Shanna and the Water Fairy:
A Beltane Story**

What is Ostara?

Ostara is a relatively new holiday celebrated by people who mark the seasons in earth-centered and Pagan beliefs. It is celebrated on March 21, a nearby weekend or whenever the spring equinox actually happens, which is sometimes on March 19 or 20. (In the southern hemisphere it is between September 21 and 23.)

The equinox is when the earth is exactly halfway between the short, cold days of winter and the long, warm days of summer. So, Ostara is a time of balance between winter and summer. In many parts of the world this is when spring really starts and there are signs of new life--buds on trees and flowers, grass sprouting, birds eggs and even baby animals--everywhere you look.

Many Easter traditions in Europe and the United States were taken from folk crafts for spring decorations, such as painting eggs. The English words Ostara and Easter both are linked to a Germanic goddess of spring called Ostre, whose symbolic animal is the hare. This and the belief that rabbits and hares are very fertile is how people got the Easter Bunny.

Celebrating Ostara is one way that Pagan families are reclaiming our own versions of folk traditions that have been absorbed into Christian holidays, such as Easter. Many earth-centered families celebrate Ostara by coloring eggs and having egg hunts. We also often have ceremonies to support new beginnings or new projects. People don't usually exchange gifts but children often get chocolate or candy.

About Arie Farnam

Arie Farnam grew up with earth-centered spirituality, She is an eclectic Pagan with a path that reflects the cultural diversity of her family as well as a deep connection to nature and ancestors.

Other than the Children's Wheel of the Year stories, she writes fantasy with Pagan themes for adults, blogs about herbs and sends out the Hearth Circle newsletter. She lives with her husband, two children and a gray cat in a house known as "the Gingerbread Cottage" just outside Prague in the Czech Republic.

About Julie Freel

Julie Freel was born into a Protestant family and taught Sunday school as a young woman. She loved the hymns, but had difficulty fully embracing the faith. She later hitchhiked to the Arizona desert and found her spirituality through a deep connection with the earth. She moved to Northeastern Oregon where she lives on Pumpkin Ridge at the edge of a unique native plant preserve.

Freel now works as a children's and family health counselor, juggles twelve grandchildren and serves as the hearth-keeper of Farnamistan. In those few moments she has free, she paints in a studio in a meadow filled with wildflowers.

CPSIA information can be obtained
at www.ICGtesting.com
Printed in the USA
LVHW071224010320
648601LV00016B/2216